SPACEBURGER

A Kevin Spoon and Mason Mintz Story

written and illustrated by Daniel Pinkwater

MACMILLAN PUBLISHING COMPANY   NEW YORK
MAXWELL MACMILLAN CANADA   TORONTO
MAXWELL MACMILLAN INTERNATIONAL   NEW YORK OXFORD SINGAPORE SYDNEY

Library of Congress Cataloging-in-Publication Data. Pinkwater, Daniel Manus, date. Spaceburger : a Kevin
Spoon and Mason Mintz story / written and illustrated by Daniel Pinkwater. — 1st ed.   p.   cm. Summary:
Kevin Spoon and Mason Mintz walk six miles to attend the opening of a new Spaceburger restaurant.
ISBN 0-02-774643-7 [1. Fast food restaurants—Fiction. 2. Restaurants—Fiction. 3. Friendship—Fiction.]
I. Title. PZ7.P6335Sp 1993   [E]—dc20   93-6658

I am Kevin Spoon. I am a normal person. I live in a normal house. I have normal parents. I go to school, where I do normal things. I dress in normal clothes. All my friends are normal friends.

Except one.

Mason Mintz is my friend. He is not a normal person. Mason Mintz
wears cheap sneakers. He wears a plaid hat. He says "Ho!" instead of "Hi!"

His parents grow pumpkins in their backyard. His mother weaves
pieces of cloth out of old string with pieces of silver foil candy wrap-
pers and beans and twigs mixed in. Then she hangs them on the wall.
His father collects stuffed owls. He has about a hundred of them.

Mason Mintz is my best friend.

One day, I was sitting on the backyard fence, listening to my portable earphone stereo. Along came Mason Mintz, down the alley that runs behind the backyards.

"Ho!" said Mason Mintz.

"You always do that," I said.

"Do what?" asked Mason Mintz.

"Say 'Ho!'" I said.

"So?" asked Mason Mintz.

"So, say 'Hi!'" I said.

"No, I say 'Ho!'" said Mason Mintz. "Ho!"

"Hi!" I said.

"Listen, Kevin Spoon," Mason Mintz said. Mason Mintz never calls me Kevin, and he never calls me Spoon. He always calls me Kevin Spoon. Actually, I like that.

"Listen, Kevin Spoon," Mason Mintz said. "On Saturday I am going to Exitville. You want to come with me?"

"Exitville? How are you going to get to Exitville?" I asked.

"Going to walk," Mason Mintz said.

"That's a long walk," I said. "Exitville must be five miles from here."

"Six," Mason Mintz said. "And six miles back."

"That's a long walk," I said. "Why do you want to go to Exitville? There's nothing there."

"Yes there is, Kevin Spoon," Mason Mintz said. "On Saturday a Spaceburger is opening in Exitville."

"A Spaceburger?"

"That's right."

"You want to walk twelve miles to go to a hamburger place?" I asked.

"A Spaceburger," Mason Mintz said.

"What for?" I asked. "There are plenty of hamburger places right here in Burbington."

"Not a Spaceburger," Mason Mintz said.

"But we've got BigBurger, Burger-Clown, Bingoburger, Belly-Burger, Bandito Burger, and Batburger," I said.

"Spaceburger is better," Mason Mintz said.

"How could it be better?" I asked. "A hamburger is a hamburger. They're all the same—a greasy piece of meat on a bun with some goo on it. Unless you mean the dinky plastic toys and cardboard hats they give away. That stuff is for babies."

"Spaceburger is better," Mason Mintz said.

"I don't see how Spaceburger can be any better than BigBurger, Burger-Clown, Bingoburger, Belly-Burger, Bandito Burger, and Batburger," I said.

"Come with me on Saturday, and see for yourself," Mason Mintz said.

"Look, Mason Mintz," I said.

"Yes, Kevin Spoon?"

"What makes you so sure that Spaceburger is better than BigBurger, Burger-Clown, Bingoburger, Belly-Burger, Bandito Burger, and Batburger, and worth a twelve-mile walk?"

"My cousin," Mason Mintz said.

"Your cousin?"

"My cousin has been to a Spaceburger in Toledo, Ohio. He told me all about it," Mason Mintz said.

"What did your cousin tell you?" I asked.

"He said that Spaceburger is *much* better than BigBurger, Burger-Clown, Bingoburger, Belly-Burger, Bandito Burger, and Batburger," Mason Mintz said.

"In what way?" I asked.

"In every way," Mason Mintz said.

"Okay, I'll go with you," I said.

"We start at six in the morning," Mason Mintz said.

"Six?"

"We don't want to get there late, Kevin Spoon."

On Saturday, Mason Mintz and I started out for Exitville. We walked in the grass along the side of the old road, which runs next to the new highway. There were hardly any cars on the highway at six in the morning—and none at all on the old road. It was quiet. We could hear the birds.

As we walked, Mason Mintz sang a song which he made up himself. It only had two words.

Lovely ravioli
Lovely ravioli
Lovely lovely lovely
Lovely ravioli

Lovely ravioli
Lovely ravioli
Lovely lovely lovely
Lovely ravioli

He sang it the whole time we were walking, and I sang it, too.

The sun got higher and warmer. A few more cars came out. We saw trees and houses and stores that had not opened yet. It was fun walking a long way, early in the morning, and singing a song about lovely ravioli.

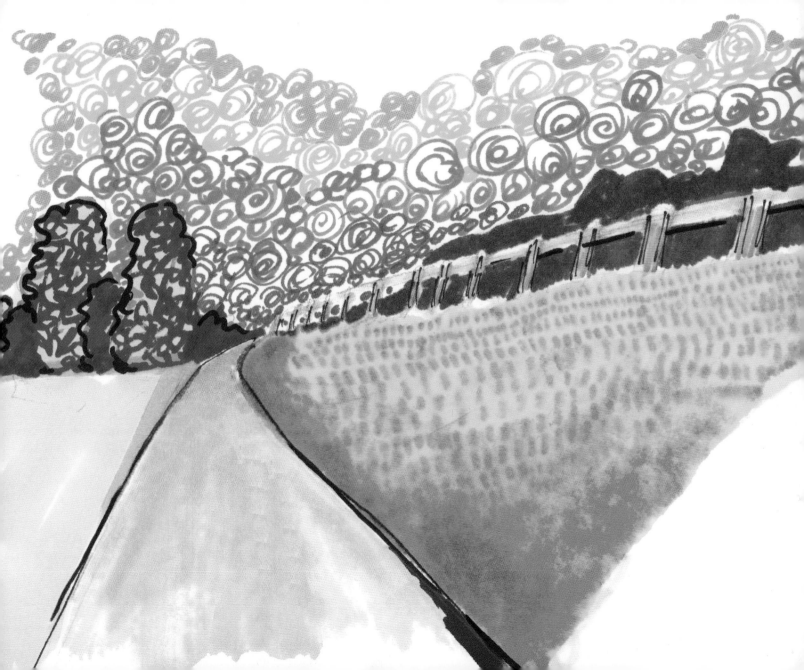

I forgot to think about the Spaceburger while we walked. It was probably just another abnormal thing that my friend Mason Mintz liked. Then, after about two hours, we saw it!

The first thing we saw was a giant silver rocket. It didn't look like a fake rocket. It looked like a real one! It was shining in the morning sun.

As we got closer, we saw that the Spaceburger itself looked like a real space station. It was the neatest thing I had ever seen.

In the parking lot was a real astronaut—or anyway someone in a real astronaut suit.

"Welcome to Spaceburger," the astronaut said. I could tell from the voice that it was a lady in the astronaut suit. "We open in three minutes, and you are our first customers."

"Perfect!" Mason Mintz said.

We looked around while we waited for the Spaceburger to open. In the drive-through lane there was an outstanding robot. The robot was the thing you talk into when you give your order.

"Hello robot," we said into the round screen thing in the robot's chest.

"Welcome to Spaceburger," the robot said, and waved to us and nodded its head. It was without a doubt the best robot I have ever seen.

Then we heard a voice come over a loudspeaker: "Spaceburger is about to open! 10–9–8–7–6–5–4–3–2–1."

We raced around to the front, and stood by the doors.

"Spaceburger is now open!"

Clouds of steam came from the bottom of the rocket as though it were taking off.

"This is the greatest thing I've ever seen," I told Mason Mintz.

Then the doors slid open, and we went in. Right inside the door was an android.

"Welcome to Spaceburger," the android said in an android voice. "You are our first customers. Please look all around, and have fun."

The android handed us each a silver card which said, FREE SPACE MEAL, then it turned and walked up the metal wall with its magnetic android shoes!

"Oh wow! This is fantastic! And we get a free space meal!" I said.

"Told you," Mason Mintz said.

We saw a sign that said: SPACE SLIDE TO THE WEIGHTLESS ROOM.

"I think that's for little kids," I told Mason Mintz.

"So what?" Mason Mintz said. "We're the only ones here."

We climbed up the ladder and slid down the space slide. It was the neatest, fastest slide I have ever been on. The weightless room wasn't really weightless, of course. But everything was padded and springy, so you could bounce everywhere, and it really did feel like floating. And there were space noises, and weird space lights. We spent a lot of time being weightless.

When we crawled out of the weightless room, we went to the counter where there were four or five aliens. We handed our FREE SPACE MEAL cards to an alien and were given two trays. Everything was wrapped in shiny silver plastic.

We carried our trays to a table, snapped on our seat belts, and unwrapped the food. It was the usual stuff you get in hamburger places, but we didn't care. Mason Mintz went back to the counter and got more packets of green space slime to put on our spaceburgers, and a few to put in our pockets.

On each tray was a neat silver space pen, which we got to keep, and a card that said:

HOW DID YOU LIKE YOUR VISIT TO
SPACEBURGER?

CHECK ONE: poor_____ fair_____ good_____ excellent _____

We both checked *excellent,* and underlined it. We handed the cards to the android who gave us each a plastic bag containing a color comic book about space science, a very decent plastic model of the rocket, and two more FREE SPACE MEAL cards.

There were a few cars coming into the parking lot as we had a last look at the robot—more early customers, but we had been the first.

Mason Mintz said, "I'd say that was completely satisfactory, wouldn't you, Kevin Spoon?"

"I couldn't agree more," I said.
And we began the long walk home,
singing the song about lovely ravioli.